For Amelie & Jack (MS)

For all my furry friends (MM)

First published in 2016 by Naughty Bird Books
www.naughtybirdbooks.com

ISBN 978-0-9935459-0-0

A CIP catalogue record for this book is available from the British Library upon request.

Layout & design by Sophie Lindsey
contact: sophielindsey@hotmail.com

Printed in the UK

The Dog from Dingle
who lost his bark

By Mark Stratton

Illustrations by Martine Moriarty

There once was a Dingle dog who lived by the sea.

His life was fun; he was happy as can be.

He liked to bark all day

and he loved to bark all night.

He was a jolly little dog

who barked with all his might.

But one fine day, when he was playing in the sun,

a great big storm came and ruined all his fun.

He ran up the beach and raced across the sand.

He was the most scared dog in all of the land.

The very next morning, when the storm had gone,
the Dingle dog realised that something was wrong!

The storm had stopped blowing and the sun was overhead,
so he tried to bark but only whimpered instead!

He thought about the rain
and how the night was dark
and realised he'd been so scared
that he'd lost his bark!

He needed to find his bark!

Where could it be?

He thought that to start,

he'd look down by the sea.

Down at the water he heard a moaning song;

he thought it was his bark, but he was wrong.

It was just a big whale playing in the kelp.

So he called out to the whale; maybe she could help.

'Excuse me Mrs Whale,' he said 'I've lost my bark.

I lost it during the storm, last night when it was dark.

I really have to find it!

Where could it be?

Oh Mrs Whale,

can you please help me?'

'Why yes, Dingle dog,' sang the whale in her song.

'I heard it in the night but I could be wrong.

There near those rocks, I heard such a strange sound.

Go look over there, my dear little hound.'

'Oh thank you,' said the Dingle dog to the great big whale

and off across the beach he ran, wagging his little tail.

Over by the rocks he heard a clicking sound,

so he stopped in his tracks and looked all around.

There was a tiny red crab clicking his claws by a boulder,

so the little dog went over and tapped his tiny shoulder.

'Excuse me Mr Crab,' he said, 'I have lost my bark.

I lost it during the storm, last night when it was dark.

I really have to find it! Where could it be?

Oh Mr Crab, can you please help me?'

'Why yes, Dingle dog,' said the crab clicking his claws.

'I heard it last night. I didn't know it was yours.

There on those cliffs I heard such a hullabaloo.

I hope you find your bark; I really, really do.'

'Oh thank you,' said the Dingle dog. 'Thanks a lot!'

And off across the sand he began to trot.

Over by the cliffs he heard a
screechy squawking.
He thought it was his bark
so instantly stopped walking.

He saw a white seagull
sitting high up on her nest,
so he shouted to the seagull
his simple request.

'Excuse me Mrs Seagull,' he said,

'I have lost my bark.

I lost it during the storm

last night when it was dark.

I really have to find it!

Where could it be?

Oh Mrs Seagull,

can you please help me?'

'Why yes, Dingle dog,' said the screechy, squawky bird.

'In the storm last night, that must have been what I heard.

There in that cave I heard such a strange commotion.

I wondered what it was; I thought it was the ocean.'

'Oh thank you!' said the dog
with a goodbye wave
and off he walked
into the big, dark cave.

Deep inside the cave there was a loud echoing roar.

He thought he may have found his bark

but could not be sure.

Instead he found a wise walrus,
who was wrinkled and old.
So he asked about his bark
and this is what he was told . . .

'Why no, Dingle doggy,
I have not seen your bark.
I expect you think you lost it
last night, when it was dark.

I know all about the storm
that passed by in the night,
and I know the wind and waves
must have given you a fright!'

'But you see, Dingle dog, you are positively wrong!

Your bark is still inside you; it's been there all along!

Summon all your courage, search deep inside your heart,

there you will find it and never will you part!'

'Oh thank you, wise walrus,' said the Dingle dog with a yelp.

'I don't know what I would have done without your thoughtful help!'

The Dingle dog thought about
what the walrus had said
and summoned all his courage
and lifted up his head.

He thought about the storm
that passed by in the night
and wanted to bark again
with all of his might.

So he ran out of the cave with the sun overhead

and he started to whimper, but then he barked instead!

He barked at Mrs Seagull and she squawked back from the sky.

He barked at Mr Crab who clicked his claws in reply.

He barked at Mrs Whale who sang back from the kelp.

He barked and he barked to thank them all for their help!

The Dingle dog continued to live by the sea.

His life was fun and he was happy as can be.

He barked in the water and barked on the sand.

He was the noisiest dog in all of the land!